KAY JAMES
MW00767833

Books in the **Today's Heroes** Series

Ben Carson

Chuck Colson

Andre Dawson

Dave Dravecky

Billy Graham

A.C. Green

Kay James

Dave Johnson

Joni's Story

Colin Powell

Becky Tirabassi

KAY JAMES

by Kay Coles James
with Jacquelline Cobb Fuller

ZondervanPublishingHouse
Grand Rapids, Michigan

A Division of HarperCollins*Publishers*

Kay James

Requests for information should be addressed to:
Zondervan Publishing House
Grand Rapids, Michigan 49530

Library of Congress Cataloging-in-Publication Data

Kay James / Kay Coles James with Jacquelline Cobb Fuller.
p. cm. — (Today's heroes)
ISBN: 0-310-49631-4 (pbk.)
1. James, Kay Coles. 2. Afro-American government executives—Biography. 3. National Right to Life Committee (U.S.)—Biography. 4. Pro-life movement—United States. 5. Abortion—United States. I. Fuller, Jacquelline Cobb. II. Title. III. Series.
E840.8.J37A3 1995 323'.092—dc20
[B] 94-45804
CIP

Edited by David Lambert

Printed in the United States of America

95 96 97 98 99 00 / ❖ LP / 10 9 8 7 6 5 4 3 2 1

Dedicated to the young ladies
of Creighton Court
in Richmond, Virginia,
and to the
Sursum Corda neighborhood
in Washington, D. C.

Contents

Chronology of Events

June 1, 1949. Madeline Kay Coles is born in Portsmouth, Virginia.

1949. Kay's family moves from Portsmouth to Richmond, where they will be closer to extended family.

1952–1953. Kay's father leaves the family and her mother struggles alone to raise six children.

1955. Kay goes to live with Aunt Pearl and Uncle J. B.

1960. Kay is one of a handful of black children who integrate Chandler Junior High School.

1966. Kay accepts Jesus Christ as her Savior after watching a Billy Graham crusade on television. Her new life as a believer begins.

1971. Kay is graduated from Hampton Institute (now University) with a degree in history and secondary education. She goes to work for C&P Telephone in Richmond and then Roanoke.

May 31, 1972. Kay meets Charles James and, within a year, they are married.

1973–1982. Kay spends time at home to raise her growing family.

1984. Charles receives a promotion, and the family, which now includes two sons and a daughter, moves to the suburbs of Washington, D.C.

1985. Kay impresses audiences with her authoritative delivery during her first televised debate on the abortion issue. Soon afterward, she is asked to join the staff of the National Right to Life.

1985. Kay becomes the Director of Public Affairs for the NRL.

1986–1988. Kay is asked by President Reagan to serve on the White House Task Force on the Black Family.

1987. Kay is appointed as a Commissioner of the National Commission on Children. President Bush later reappoints her to this position.

1988. Kay speaks to the Republican National Convention in New Orleans and introduces Senator William Armstrong of Colorado.

1988. Kay resigns from NRL to care for her mother, who is diagnosed with cancer.

1989. Kay joins the Bush Administration as Assistant Secretary for Public Affairs at the U.S. Department of Health and Human Services.

1991. Kay becomes Senior Vice President and Chief Operating Officer of the One-to-One Foundation, a nonprofit organization dedicated to building mentoring relationships between business persons and youth.

1991. President Bush asks Kay to serve as Associate Director for the White House Office of National Drug Control Policy.

1992. Kay speaks at the Republican National Convention in Dallas and introduces Governor Voinovich of Ohio.

1993. Kay becomes Senior Vice President of the Family Research Council, a Washington-based policy organization.

1993. Zondervan Books publishes *Never Forget*, the story of Kay's life.

1994. Kay becomes the Secretary of Health and Human Resources for Governor Allen of Virginia, where she is responsible for health care and welfare reform policies, as well as the management of nineteen thousand employees and a budget of four billion dollars.

1

I Will Never Forget

It was the summer of 1985, and the James Gang was touring the nation's capital, where we had lived for several years. On this particular day, Charles and I with eleven-year-old Chuck, ten-year-old Elizabeth, and seven-year-old Robbie were waiting in line to tour George Washington's home at Mount Vernon. It was hot and humid, and Robbie had to go to the bathroom. The older children were clearly displaying an I'd-rather-be-shopping-at-an-air-conditioned-mall look. Robbie kept pestering us about finding a bathroom, but I wanted him to wait until we had toured the estate. I tried to put him off by telling him that there were no bathrooms at Mount Vernon.

"There must be one someplace," he asserted. "George Washington had to go to the bathroom, too."

The family ahead in line all giggled at Robbie's insight. We were a fairly even match. The dad was reading a brochure, the mom stood with two or three grade-school children, and a teenager stood with hands on hips, complaining about the heat. Picking up on Robbie's brazen comment, they pestered their parents with questions about life in George Washington's day.

"Did he have any kids? Did they play football? Did they ride horses?"

One question, however, caught my attention:

"How in the world did George mow all this lawn?" the young son asked.

His simple question held an opportunity to lay open a great, neglected truth about some of our founding fathers: These men who fought so hard for the cause of liberty also owned slaves. George Washington, in fact, once sold a slave to Thomas Jefferson. I strained to hear how the mother would answer this loaded question.

"Oh, I don't know," she sighed. "It must have taken him a long time."

I was disappointed by her reply because I

was quite sure that George Washington had never cut a blade of grass, washed a dish, or cooked a meal himself! I began a history lesson for my kids in a voice loud enough to be heard by the family next to us: "You know, kids, George Washington was a very powerful man in his time. The Mount Vernon estate stretched out over eight thousand acres, and he owned many slaves. The slaves hunted and fished for food; they cleaned the house and kept fires burning; they tended the gardens, worked the fields. Slave women spun flax and wool into cloth, and cooked and baked food in the kitchen. Some slaves worked as carpenters and blacksmiths and built most of the buildings we're going to see today at Mount Vernon.

"It was the sweat of your ancestors," I explained to my children, "that earned Mount Vernon its name. But unlike the gardeners and groundskeepers of today, they weren't allowed to receive financial reward for the work they had done."

I went on to explain that although he had held strong convictions about freedom, George Washington and most others of his era reserved these rights for white men. Women couldn't vote. Native Americans couldn't vote. Slaves couldn't vote. Only white men who owned land were entrusted with voting privileges in Virginia.

"George Washington had second thoughts later. He gave his slaves their freedom in his will. He also asked that the freed slaves be taught to read and write and trained in a useful occupation."

My two older children, Chuck and Elizabeth, seemed to catch on to the significance of my history lesson. They nodded and looked out over the carefully manicured gardens. For them—and, I hoped, for the family ahead of us—the beauty of the estate took on a new meaning.

Robbie, on the other hand, wanted to know where the slaves went to the bathroom.

2

Humble Beginnings

My father and brothers weren't home the sultry June night that I was born. They were hunting bullfrogs in the swamp out back with flashlights and burlap sacks. Ten-year-old Ted had stuffed about as many in his sack as his daddy had. The other sons, Peter and Lucky, were still too young to be of much use, but they went along to shine the flashlight when the others went in for a catch. They would also hold the light on the critters when Daddy used the ax from the woodshed to cut off the hindquarters. The boys were looking forward to bringing them home to Mama, who would shake the frog legs in a bag with flour, salt, and pepper, and then sear them in oil.

Home was a salty stretch of land in the black section of Portsmouth, Virginia. The only black doctor in town couldn't be located to deliver me. A neighbor brought me into the kitchen to wash me off and then laid my crying self on the kitchen table for all the males in the family to marvel at.

And marvel they did at the little girl who had followed four boys. I would be the only one of six children to wear pink. My daddy used to like excuses to drink, so he said, "A baby girl! I'll drink to that!" And he did—for the next thirty years.

I was the third Coles baby to be born at 94 Carver Circle, a humble old house with linoleum floors and peeling, painted walls. Our neighborhood was a series of small houses that had been converted from army barracks after the war. It had all the charm of a cement mixer.

The house was a tight fit for the Coles family. Only two bedrooms—one for my parents and me, and another for the four boys. But my brothers were usually outdoors crabbing, gathering wood, or playing in the woods. The only time my mother was really pressed to have a bigger home was when she was pregnant and her tiny four-foot-seven-inch frame became as wide as it was tall.

The neighborhood was as cozy as the houses, with hardly room enough between them to stretch a laundry line. Mama's best friend was her next-door neighbor, a round-figured woman who loved to come and sip lemonade with my folks on the porch. She and Daddy became friendly. Real friendly. My father ended up marrying that woman later in life.

My father, along with most of the men in the neighborhood, worked at the navy yard as a longshoreman.The money bought food and clothing, but it also bought liquor. And the liquor brought pain. My brothers later told me about the vicious verbal spats that my father and mother would have over his drinking.

My father was a man who wanted more than a black man in his day could have: a job utilizing his talents and skills, a paycheck big enough to feed his wife and children, respect from the white man. None of these things came easily in the segregated South of the forties and fifties. The work at the yards was good while it lasted, but it didn't last long. He took very hard his inability to provide for us and hid his failure in long sips of whiskey.

I remember the gentle strokes that he saved for the face of his only daughter. And I remember, too, his drinking and how drastically his personality changed when his breath smelled of whiskey.

Life in Portsmouth proved a trying time for my mother. She was a simple woman, as simple as her name, Sue. In her mind there were very few things in life worth getting "fussed up about," but family was one of them. The youngest of six girls of a prominent family, she was treated as the baby. She was wholly unprepared for life as a mother of six, with an alcoholic husband.

There were many discussions over Sunday dinner among relatives in Richmond on what to do about sister Sue, whose no-good husband wasn't taking care of her or the children. Shortly after I was born, one of Mama's sisters, Pearl, and her husband, J. B., came down to Portsmouth, packed up Mama and the five children and brought us back to Richmond. I was three months old at the time, too young to notice the "I told you so" that was in the air if not on their lips. Mama had shocked and disappointed the family when she and my father dropped out of college to marry, especially since they didn't "have to."

We moved in with Great-great-aunt Duk in a rickety Victorian home. It was a huge house whose many dark, musty rooms were a playground for ghoulish fascinations. It was so big and scary; there were rooms my brothers didn't even go into the whole three years we lived there. We never wandered into old Aunt Duk's room, a sunless back room off the second floor at the end of a long and lonesome hallway.

To this day my brothers are convinced that house was visited by haunts and ghouls who had some sort of relationship with the old matriarch of the house who (we kids suspected) was really a witch. Aunt Duk certainly looked the part. Age had taken some of her height, and what she had left bent over like a wilted violet. Her skin was shriveled and hung in loose folds from her bony frame. She had habits that scared the boys, like spending the day holed up in her room alone only to come out at night to creep down the hallways for no particular reason.

Fear made us an even closer bunch of siblings. There were no complaints when Mama instructed us to do all of our playing in the large downstairs living room during the cold winter months. It was only at night that we'd venture upstairs to slip into our beds, whose sheets Mama had warmed with an iron. The fire that Peter and Ted would stoke sputtered out some time near midnight, and the winter chill would seep into our floors and bedposts.

"Good-night, sleep tight, don't let Jack Frost get you tonight," Mama would say as she tucked us into bed. And we would pull the warm sheet up to our chin and try not to move all night lest some of the cold air find its way down to our toes. During the Christmas season and the frosty months following, we could see our breath as we whispered good-nights into the bedroom air. During that season Mama would pile coats, clothes, and old towels on top of us to help keep us warm as we lay in bed. None of us minded being doubled and tripled up in bed then. The more bodies the warmer—and the better.

The older boys had chores around the house, which they would dutifully perform while we younger ones followed at a respectful distance and observed. I especially remember Ted's jobs of feeding the pet chickens he kept on the second-floor balcony and keeping the fire lit in the coal furnace.

One morning as we toddled around after Ted, my younger brother Arthur opened up the furnace as he had just seen his older brother do, and he stuck his face in the opening. The next second, the whole house echoed with the blast from the exploding furnace. Ted hollered out the Lord's name in a blast almost as loud as the explosion as he pulled his soot-faced little brother away from the furnace. Arthur's eye-brows were burned right off his face. We knew that someone was going to get it, not because we had let Arthur burn himself but because someone had used the Lord's name in vain.

Mama, who called out to God routinely through her exclamations, had absolutely no tolerance for those who called upon the Lord in a disrespectful manner. As my brothers got older, if a "damn" or a "hell" slipped out after spending a little too much time with their father, they could expect a quick reprimand. But if you *ever* took the Lord's name in vain, you'd better duck!

* * *

Like all mothers, Mama had words to live by. These sayings hinted at the homegrown faith in Jesus that was as much a part of her as her broad smile and smoky brown skin. "Lord, have mercy!" was her response to just about anything alarming or interesting. "Mama, ain't no more flour in the bin," one of us would say. "Lord, have mercy!" she'd say. Another child would say,

"Mama, I got an A on my spelling test." "Lord, have mercy!" Mama would answer with a smile lighting her angelic face.

I knew that I could count on greens at Sunday dinner, baths on Saturday night, and Mama's always taking the six of us to church on Sundays (my little brother, Tony, was born after the family returned to Richmond). Baths were taken in a round tub in the kitchen. Each child had his turn and then Tony and I would get in together. Each night before bed, Mama required us to get on our knees to say our prayers. Once when the cold of winter seeped through the wooden floor, Lucky dared to complain about this ritual. Mama quickly cut him off: "Son, you get on your feet to play football, you crouch in the bushes to play tag, you can sure enough get on your knees to pray to your God!" That was the last time any of us complained about kneeling for prayer.

Life on Second Street was marked by a fear and insecurity that had less to do with the ghouls we imagined than with the fights we witnessed between our parents. There was a battle warring in Daddy's soul between his love for his family and his craving for drink. "You better stop with that whiskey," Mama would say with tired hope. "It's going to kill you someday!" But Daddy would brush off her concern: "I know it, but I'm gonna drink it till the day I die."

Fighting words began to take the place of conversation between my parents, and Daddy's threats of violence turned into slaps and punches. We younger children were shielded from his brutality, but Mama and the older boys bore on their bodies the heaviness of his rage. The tension between my parents was hardest on Ted, the oldest child and the one who stood in for Daddy when he couldn't perform his duties as head of the household.

Ted got the idea that if only Mama and the kids could get away from Daddy, then everything would be all right. One morning when most of the kids were out playing, Ted and Mama were alone in the kitchen. As soon as she went into the living room to do her mending, he stole up the steps to one of the bedrooms. There in the secrecy of the dark, he set a mattress on fire and slipped back downstairs.

Smoke began to filter down the steps as he played with Arthur and me under Mama's watchful eyes, but no one noticed the gray cloud descending the stairs. Ted was bouncing me on his knees and his nervousness made for an especially bumpy ride, but still no one but Ted noticed the acrid smell. When he saw the flames

starting to lick the banister and that still no one had noticed, he finally yelled, "Mama, the house is on fire!" and the four of us ran out the back door. Firemen were soon on the scene.

Then Ted suddenly remembered his chickens on the second-story balcony. He was off like a cat, running straight for the burning house. We were all very relieved to see him emerge from the back door a few moments later, with three soot-blackened chickens flapping in his arms.

Ted hadn't succeeded in burning down the house. For all the excitement the mysterious fire had generated in the neighborhood, the flames had only damaged a few rooms and a mattress—but his underlying purpose, to free Mama and the kids from his sometimes violently abusive father, was achieved. It was only a few short months after the fire that Mama left Daddy for good and moved us into a public-housing project called Creighton Court.

3

Creighton Court

My first impression of the "projects," as we called them, was of pleasant-looking buildings surrounded by grass and playgrounds. Once inside however, it lost all of its humanity. In each of the five rooms, rough gray cinder-block walls met an equally dreary concrete floor. The worst adjustment was to our new roommates: hundreds and hundreds of cockroaches! They would crawl up the drain in the bathtub and find their way into virtually every nook and cranny in the apartment.

One advantage of having five brothers was

that Mom and I could call on them to come kill the roaches that we spotted on the table or in the silverware drawer. Often as I lay in bed at night, I would fight sleep, worrying that one of the brown creepers would fall from the ceiling and crawl around on my face as I slept. Each night there was a ritual that I would perform religiously. After brushing my teeth, I would get on my knees and say my prayers out loud for Mama to hear. After pulling back the sheets to check for any wayward bugs, I'd sing songs to myself to take my mind off the roaches that came out when the light went off. Each morning I would check my shoes before putting them on, to make sure that none had taken up residence in them the night before.

"The insect problem," as Mama referred to our roaches, was accepted as part of life in a public-housing complex. Winter nights were spent doubled and tripled up in bed. Because I was the smallest, I usually ended up in a bed with at least two brothers. I loved to press my cold nose against their warm necks and giggle as they yipped and shivered. I felt safe, and warm, and loved. As we huddled in bed together, I thought of all the poor boys and girls who didn't have brothers or sisters they could snuggle with in bed. "Lord, bless the children who don't have anyone to sleep with to keep them warm at night," I'd whisper on my way toward sleep.

My friends and I filled the sidewalks with chalk pictures of cats and frogs and smiling faces, but our masterpieces never lasted long because the boys in the neighborhood ignored our protests and walked over them, smudging the figures into white clouds.

Because we lived in subsidized housing, we were called "project" kids—the bottom of the pecking order in Richmond. Even the black kids who lived up on the "hill"—the more affluent black neighborhood—called us "project niggers." We knew no sweeter thrill than beating one of the hill kids at double-dutch, kickball, baseball, tag, or football.

Football games were the centerpiece of our competitions. Both sides would spend weeks practicing in the hot afternoon sun, devising elaborate plays for the big game. On the day of the match, the hill team would show up with shoulder pads, cloth helmets, and cleats. Our team was doing well if everyone showed up with shoes. I don't think that my brothers ever understood why God blessed the hill kids doubly: Not only did they come from families with money, but they were incredible athletes as well.

Our rivalry with the well-to-do hill kids

instilled in my brothers and me an us-against-them mentality. We were determined to prove that we were just as smart, just as fast, just as good as they were. This drive to excel was sharpened by an awareness of being the black sheep of our extended family.

My mother was an Armistead, one of a handful of well-respected families in Richmond. The Armistead sisters earned their good name by going to college, holding interesting jobs, and marrying well. All, that is, except Mama. The youngest of five sisters, she was treated as the baby, pampered, and protected. Perhaps that's why she so easily fell for my handsome, charming, and chronically jobless father.

We may have been black sheep and project niggers to others, but to Mama we were precious children expected to live up to her high standards. One time Peter dared to talk back to Mama. Now Mama was only four-foot-seven, and she had a difficult time smacking the boys once they crossed the six-foot mark. But on this occasion, Mama pushed Lucky's box of marbles right off the edge of the counter. "Boy, pick those marbles up." As he bent over to pick them up, Mama bopped him upside the head.

And we knew better than to disrespect any of the other adults in the community, either. If

Mr. Lincoln next door said, "Son, I don't think that's something your mama would want you to be doing," you knew that you'd best not do it. The neighborhood was filled with people like Aunt Nervy. That woman whipped us more often than our own mother did. I never have quite figured out who she was. I don't think she was even a relative. She'd never threaten us with "I'll tell your mama!"—she took care of business right there on the spot. And you sure enough weren't going to go home talking about, "Mama, Aunt Nervy hit me!" 'cause you knew that Mama would flare her nostrils and say, "For what?" And bop, you'd get it again.

These extra sets of parents and kin in the neighborhood could be a real asset. If it weren't for Mrs. Gladys next door, I'd have gone through my entire childhood with my hair in a ponytail. With five boys, Mama wasn't much on doing hair, so she used to take me over to Mrs. Gladys, who knew how to do all sorts of braids and twists.

I enjoyed the chaotic hustle-bustle of children running through the house and was never bored because I always had a playmate at hand. Even though my father was gone more than he was home, I never really felt a void, because in my world there were so many others loving me and providing care. Creighton Court had several families with neglected kids—children who didn't have anyone who thought that they were special. I knew that I was someone special because I always had my hair done nicely. Why would Mrs. Gladys waste her time doing someone's hair if that person was poor and worthless? I may have been hungry and poor, but I was *neat-and-clean* hungry and poor.

Periodically, something that seemed especially evil would invade the relative security of our neighborhood. It came hidden behind white hoods and was known by its frightening initials: KKK. They held their cross burnings in the field that we sometimes used for football games, not even half a mile down the street next to the police station. It used to scare me to death when cars filled with yoo-hooing hooded whites drove down Nine-Mile Road, headed for the big rally. It never was clear in my mind that they hated us because we were black. I didn't understand racism. I just knew that they were evil people who would hurt a little girl if she was caught alone near the field on a rally night. One time Ted didn't get the word that it was rally night, and he went out to pick blackberries in the woods by the field. He had to hide in a bush when two hooded figures with shotguns walked right by him.

Our boundaries were strictly marked off. Never was I to cross Nine-Mile Road, the busy two-lane street that passed in front of our building and intersected Bunche Place. Because the other side of Nine-Mile Road was off-limits, the grass there was a vibrant green that took on its own light when the sun danced upon it. Unlike the stamped-down, limp, yellow grass that spotted the dirt in the play area out back, this grass was tall and willowy and left paths of darker green when the wind swept by.

One day after inspecting our sorry patch of dirt out back, Tony and I decided that it would be much more fun to play across the street. An idea popped into my head that seemed the perfect plan. If you followed Bunche Place long enough down the block, it ended in a cul-de-sac. Therefore, I reasoned, one could follow along the edge of the road, curve along the cul-de-sac and be safely on the other side. I grabbed Tony's hand, and we skipped around till we were on the other side of the busy street. We flopped on our backs and began wiggling our arms and legs to make angels in the grass.

The sound of a slamming screen door across the street brought us to our senses. It was Mama, and she was headed straight for us with a full head of steam. She strode toward us, hitching up her dress midstep with one hand, pumping the air with the other to pick up speed.

"Lord, have mercy!" I mumbled with my heart in my throat, and I began to cry in anticipation of the spanking that her eyes told me I was soon to receive. We were barely on our feet before Mama nabbed us and began yanking us toward home.

"How many times have I told you not to cross Nine-Mile Road?" she asked, not waiting for an answer. The more Tony and I tried to explain that we hadn't really crossed the street, the angrier she got. She began spanking both of us with strong underhand strokes.

After Mama had settled down, we finally were able to explain how we got across the street without really *crossing* the street. Then Mama got so upset for spanking us that *she* began crying. She called us, and pretty soon we were all hugging each other as Tony patted her on the back and told her that it was all right.

4

Project Niggers

We watched Mama board a bus in the cold morning hours and return after sunset, tired but ready to cook and clean for her own family. Her daily routine taught us the dignity of honest work. When we were tempted to turn to unchristian activities to sweeten the dullness of a no-frills life, Mama always reminded us that we were better than that. If we were dying to have something that was the rage among the other kids, no amount of whining to Mama would get it. If we wanted it, she would tell us, “Go out and get a job to pay for it.”

These principles of living applied even when our sparse diet of chicken and biscuits was cut back to "fatback" and biscuits. A standard dinner was Hungarian goulash—Mama's name for hamburger meat with canned spaghetti and any leftovers in the refrigerator. It used to kill us on Sunday afternoons to walk home for dinner across the neighborhood and smell fried chicken wafting through the air.

Some of Ted's friends figured out that the kitchen at the elementary school could be broken into fairly easily. Now Ted was a tagalong, and he went along with them when they broke into the school's walk-in refrigerator and stole some of the plucked chickens hanging there for school lunches.

You can imagine our joy (and surprise) to see Ted come in the back door with his hands full of chickens. We started jumping up and down and doing something like a square dance right there in the kitchen. None of us asked him where he got them, knowing somewhere in the back of our minds that it'd be best not to. But there was no sense in trying to fool Mama once she got home. She knew that Ted hadn't bought the chickens, but she waited to hear his story.

He just flat out told her he had taken them from the school, banking on the fact that she would see it as he did: not really stealing, since the school seemed such an impersonal storehouse. She took those chickens by the feet and started pummeling Ted, who was ducking left and right, trying to avoid getting poked with a wing or a bill. She backed him into a corner and, with one hand still holding the birds and the other pointed right in his face, she spoke in a voice so low and forceful that you'd have thought that God was speaking: "Boy! I will *starve* before I let one of my children bring stolen food into this house."

That was all she said before she turned and opened the back door. We all watched bug-eyed as she flung those chickens into the backyard.

My brothers and I remembered that incident whenever anyone from another part of town called us "project niggers." Because of Mama's high standards, we knew who we were. We might have grown up in a public housing project, but Mama *raised* us at home.

Aunt Pearl and Uncle J. B. began bringing me out to their home more and more. Often I would stay overnight and eventually every weekend. I looked forward to these times away from all the noise and confusion of our apartment.

We followed a routine. First, my hair would be rebraided and then Aunt Pearl would tell me to go put on one of the made-to-wear dresses that she had bought for me at a store. I was only five at the time, and her doting attention made me believe that perhaps fairy godmothers really do exist and that she was mine.

On these visits I truly felt like a princess. Not only did I have my own room, I had my very own bed! It was the first time that I had ever slept in a bed without at least two of my brothers. *How had I gotten so lucky?* I wondered, and I made a pledge to thank God every night for His goodness to me.

Then one afternoon Mama called me into the kitchen and gave me the news. As she set me up on her lap, close to her bosom as she did on the few occasions when she did my hair, I knew that something was wrong. Her tear-swollen eyes confirmed my hunches.

"Child, opportunity don't come knocking but so many times in a person's life ... You know that, don't you, Kay?"

"Yes, ma'am," I murmured.

"Well," she continued, "your Aunt Pearl and Uncle J. B., because they love you so much and want to provide opportunities for you ..."

Pause.

"They want you to go and live with them."

There it was. The dagger had struck, and I

felt my heart bleeding inside of me. Words would not come out—only tears and a muffled moan.

"Now Kay, Pearl and J. B. can give you things that your mama could never give you. You'll be able to go on vacations. You'll be able to have nice clothes, even go to college one day." With every item that she added to the list, I shook my head in rejection.

"No, Mommy, I want to stay with you and my brothers and ..." She didn't say any more. I lay against her and cried in defiant silence. I didn't want new clothes and college. I wanted to be with my family.

Soon the voices of my aunt and uncle floated up through the still night air to where I had shut myself in the bedroom. Mama was making small talk, waiting for me to answer her call for me to come downstairs, but I couldn't move. My legs were pulled up tight against my chest, molding my body into a ball on the bed.

"Kay, darling." It was Mama. Her voice was softer than I had ever heard it. It sounded as smooth and gentle as the velour coverings on the pews in church. She pulled me up on my knees, and we sat on the bed looking swollen eye to swollen eye.

"Little boys can play in the gutter and get up the next morning, put on a clean shirt, and nobody thinks anything of it, because they're boys. A little girl ..." She paused and touched me gently on the cheek. "A little girl can play in the gutter and get up the next morning, and everybody remembers. And I want you out of this gutter. This is an opportunity for you. I'm still your mama and I will always be your mama, but you're going to take advantage of these opportunities. They're going to give you things that I can't give you."

"Yes ma'am," I answered between sniffles, and I packed my few things and went downstairs. I never questioned my mother's love for me. I trusted her completely, but my heart ached at the thought of leaving my family and neighbors and everything that my small world contained at that time. But Sue Coles had spoken, and I obeyed.

Aunt Pearl was ecstatic, and even Uncle J. B. had difficulty subduing his elation at seeing me come down the stairs with my bag. I hugged each of my brothers good-bye. As the Chrysler pulled away, I watched through blurry eyes as Creighton Court melted into Nine-Mile Road.

We went directly to the Sears store, where I was outfitted with an entirely new wardrobe. Panties, slips, dresses, socks—nothing was left out. At my new home, my aunt and I unpacked my new clothes and arranged them in neat rows in my dresser. And so I went to bed, feeling like a princess. I didn't have to fight sleep, because no cockroaches crawled across the ceiling in my new house. I stretched my legs out to the edges of the bed, enjoying the coolness of the fresh sheets against my skin and the freedom of not having to jostle with my brothers for leg room or covers. It was so still and quiet that I wouldn't have to hum songs to drown out the sound of hollering in another apartment. I should have been the happiest girl in the world, but for the first time in my life I felt very lonely and very alone. I cried. The more I tried to suck in my sobs, the more my tiny body shook with the heaving motions of my crying. After a while the sobs turned into a low and mournful moan as I cried softly into my pillow until I drifted off to sleep.

As sad as it was to leave Mama, I had at least two things going for me. First, I was still with family. Pearl and J. B. were not strangers but familiar faces from a wonderful extended family. And in our community it wasn't unusual for family to take care of each other.

Second, Pearl and J. B. had several surprises for me that made the transition a little easier. One of the things I was most excited about was that they were going to wallpaper their home and I got to pick out the wallpaper for my room. That was one of the most exciting things that had happened to me in my short life. I picked out a bubblegum-pink print of ballerinas. For the rest of my time in that house, I lived with pink, fluffy ballerinas all over my walls.

There were only three of us in a four-bedroom house, and it took me a long time to get used to having so much space and so much quiet. I missed my family, but it was a pain that I learned to live with, like a toothache whose dull hurt is so often with you that you learn to ignore it. We still saw one another quite often. My brother Lucky came over on weekends to do heavy cleaning for my aunt. I'd sit and talk to him while he scrubbed floors, washed down the woodwork, or did yard work.

These were to be years of pain and struggle for me—years of growth. My eyes were opened to the dividing lines of American society. I became aware that there were haves and have-nots, "niggers" and white folks, professionals and servants, men and women. I questioned why God had put me on the weaker side of every one of the lines I discovered. For the first time, I saw how the other half lived, and I realized that we were desperately poor. And I heard day after day that we Coles were the black sheep of the family. These discoveries came when I was removed from an environment that, for all its cockroaches and material want, was still a pleasant home.

5

The Hothouse

There was a firm conviction among black folks that education was our avenue to freedom. Mothers, fathers, grandparents, neighbors, pastors, everyone took an interest in our schoolwork. This academic focus was heightened in my case because my aunt was a schoolteacher herself. Every morning I tagged along with her to attend Webster Davis, where she taught, rather than the school near our house.

The environment of Webster Davis worked quite a change in me from the time I entered Junior Primary One to when I graduated from the sixth grade. Of all the adjectives used to describe me today, I don't think that anyone has ever chosen the word "passive." As a black woman who is both an evangelical Christian and a pro-life Republican, my life could hardly be described as easygoing.

As a child, though, I was so nonconfrontational that in the first grade I sat there and let a little girl cut off one of my braids. That night, staring at the bushy nub that marked the place where my shoulder-length braid had been, Aunt Pearl asked incredulously, "Why'd you let her do that? Why didn't you say anything?" I still don't know the answer to that question, but something almost mystical happened during the six years I spent at Webster Davis, and by the time I reached the sixth grade, I was president of the student body.

Much of the transformation can be attributed to people like Elsie Lewis, the principal of Webster Davis. In the 1950s there were few opportunities for educated blacks to get jobs, so it was not unusual to have black teachers with Ph.D.s teaching elementary school. Our segregated junior high schools used secondhand textbooks, but a black man with a Ph.D. in chemistry taught science class.

At that point in my life I had had so little firsthand experience with white folks that my understanding of them came almost entirely from my teachers. They told us that white kids were given all the breaks and advantages and that we had to be better than them to be treated equally. We were told in no uncertain terms that we had to be twice as good and twice as smart to survive. I can recall my sixth grade teacher, Mrs. Waltz, pointing her ramrod-straight arm up the hill to the white elementary school, Fulton Hill. "Those kids are going to be waiting for you when you get out of here," she would intone, and with eyes flashing she would add, "and you are going to be ready!"

At Webster Davis you never heard children complaining to their teachers that such-and-such was not fair. We knew that such objections would get us nowhere. "Life is not fair" I heard many a teacher snap, "and so don't go looking for fair." We accepted the inherent difficulties and injustices of life as we accepted the stifling humidity of Richmond summers. We didn't like it, and we stiffened our resolve to fight against it, but we conditioned ourselves to persevere and thrive in spite of it. And we knew with a knowing so deep that they must have seasoned the water fountains with it, that life was going to be tough. No one at Webster Davis ever led us to believe that we could expect to get anything in life that we didn't sweat, bleed, and work for.

But even as our teachers painted us a realistic picture of black life in the fifties, they held up examples of those who had gone before us who had triumphed when the world was even more unfair. They filled our heads with the lyrical prose of James Baldwin. We read biographies of bold and courageous Harriet Tubman and Nat Turner, and the ingenious George Washington Carver. At Webster Davis we learned that we were part of a proud race of survivors. If I tried to explain away my not doing my algebra homework because of the heavy weight of years of slavery, a heavy weight would soon come down on my behind!

These lessons were reinforced at home with a religious fervor. Every day when I came home from school, I was required to spread out my books in the "breakfast nook." There I pored over my lessons, hour after hour. I always had two companions sitting with me: Aunt Pearl and her can of beer. I would begin these homework sessions with English, my favorite subject, and save math for last. I had a very definite reason for doing so. My aunt would look over every assignment, checking for errors. This review was helpful at first, but by the time the last two or three subjects

came around, Pearl would be so tipsy that she did little more than ramble and berate me.

She would crumple up my math homework and screech at me that I had done them all wrong. The problems were easy enough to check in my head so I could know for sure that my answers were correct. I would redo the problems again and again, each time Pearl insisting that I was such an "ignorant fool" that I had answered every one wrong, until eventually she would relent and say that I'd finally gotten them right.

My head was so packed full of learning by the end of the school year that I was desperate for summer to come. Summer camps are an invention of modern times to give urban kids a chance to get out of the city and experience the joy of life in the country. When we were growing up, black kids didn't need summer camps because everyone had family in the country.

After school let out, the exodus began as kids were shipped out to spend the season with any kin that lived in the country. When we came back together in the fall, we traded stories about milking cows, castrating hogs, and building forts in the woods. We were lucky. My uncle J. B. had a brother and a sister who lived nearby in New Kent County. Every summer we spent weekends and odd days at their farm. My relatives in New

York City sent their kids down for the entire summer. We city kids relished the playgrounds that Mother Nature had created for our cousins. The country was a world of wonder for those of us who thought that milk came from a truck and that vegetables grew in supermarkets. We caught tadpoles in the brook and climbed trees and chased rabbits.

Meals in the country were a celebration. The food was good and plentiful. They ate Sunday dinner every day: fresh vegetables, succotash, ham, peach pie, and other things that we ate only on special occasions at home. The exercise, fresh air, and Southern home-cooking left me healthy and refreshed for another school year. It also provided a desperately needed break from the demands of living up to Aunt Pearl's expectations.

All too soon it was time to return to Richmond and the rigors of school. Looking back, I am very thankful for that time in the hothouse, for it strengthened my roots and extended my branches and, in general, prepared me for a time when I would be transplanted to a foreign soil within my own country—white-people land. Had it not been for those nurturing years, I may very well have wilted and faded under the scorching heat of racial injustice that I would soon experience in white America.

6

Tossing the Salad

My clothes for my first day of junior high school had been carefully ironed and starched. My brand-new saddle shoes were a gleaming black and white, without a single crease in the leather. Pearl and I spent a long time picking out just the right dress. I was more nervous on my first day at Chandler Junior High School than I had been leaving for Junior Primary One. We were going from being the leaders of grade school to lowly seventh graders.

Even worse, some man had taken the school system to court, and the judge had decided that schools should be integrated. I wondered why integration meant that black students were thrust into white territory. Integration *never* meant that white girls left their friends and neighborhoods to attend a black school like Webster Davis.

Frankly, this tossing of the proverbial salad bowl of American cultures was an unwelcome nuisance. On May 17, 1954, the U.S. Supreme Court outlawed segregation (separating people by race) in public schools. Six years later, the first group of black children was sent out in groups of twos and threes to integrate schools where they were outnumbered a hundred to one.

Some parents were so upset by the thought of their kids sitting beside black children that they withdrew their children from public schools. We feared there might be violence. I was one of twenty-six black students joining the incoming class of three hundred white students at Chandler.

I felt overwhelmed. I walked softly down the halls, my head turned down, intimidated by the older kids towering above me. In the hallways I backed my skinny, undeveloped body against the wall so that I did not have to answer the conceited stares of the girls who had sprouted breasts and the boys who smoked cigarettes behind the school dumpster.

The always noisy, always frantic corridors provided cover for white bullies. For the first month, I never made it from one class to the next without at least one student pricking me with a pin. Sometimes I was stuck so many times I had to press my dress against my body to keep the red streams from dripping down my legs. I tried to be discreet. I didn't want them to know that their taunts or their jabs hurt me.

At first I couldn't tell one white student from the rest. They all looked and dressed pretty much the same. Even the ones who didn't jab us never talked to us. The black kids had been spread out one or two to a class. We sought each other out during lunch and sat together in one big black clump. That was the only time I felt safe. The rest of the day I was afraid and alone.

My greatest fear was being caught alone in the hallway with one of the toughs who took special joy in threatening us. One day it happened. I was descending a large stairway when a group of white kids started up. Most of them ignored me as I tried to step down the side. But one of them waited till my back was turned and pushed me, hard, down the stairs. I landed at the end with my shins and back bruised. Apparently it wasn't

enough for him, so he kicked my books all over the hall as well. The crowd laughed and made jokes.

And then an amazing thing happened. A girl whom I had never even spoken with before, stepped out and began helping me gather my books. She continued even as her friends turned on her and called her "nigger lover." Unfazed, she walked me down the hall to the office. She didn't say much, but she said enough to make it clear that the boy who pushed me spoke and acted for himself, and not for all white people. I will never forget her act of courage.

Hallways were scary, but once into my next class I could breathe a sigh of relief. I instinctively trusted the teachers. I sat close to the front where they could see that I was sitting up straight, paying attention, and ready to answer their questions. One day during homeroom, my teacher read off the menu: "Today we're having grilled cheese sandwiches, vegetable soup, milk, and brownies for dessert." At this point she paused and looked over her glasses at me and added for the class's enjoyment, "And heaven knows why they're having brownies. We have enough of them here already."

That remark stung more than the pinpricks I had received in the halls. I expected taunts from the students, but I had imagined that if things ever got really bad, we could go to the teachers who would protect us. But I was a "brownie" in Mrs. Osborne's eyes, and there was no safe haven at John Chandler.

I went on to John Marshall High School where things were not much different. Life at home was often worse. Aunt Pearl could be kind, generous, and fun to be with. And she was so dedicated to her teaching that she never went to school tipsy, or reeling from a hangover. But every day after school Pearl would begin drinking, and the perfect Armistead would soon become another person. As I passed from junior to senior high, her tongue-lashings got meaner.

"You aren't going to amount to a thing! The Coles blood in you is going to ruin you!" I learned most of what I knew about rebellion from her fantasies about what I was supposedly doing. "You stumbling around like you been drinking!" she'd spew at me, her breath covering my face with an alcohol cloud. "And I smell smoke on you, too, you sorry little cheat. You been smoking cigarettes with those boyfriends of yours, now ain't you?"

At times she would become so agitated, imagining my sins, that she would kick me out of the house! One time when my uncle was out of town, Aunt Pearl threw all of my clothes out in the front yard and put me out like a cat on the doorstep.

It occurred to me one Saturday, as I was holed up in my room with the pink ballerinas on the walls, that I might as well indulge myself. If was going to be punished for drinking, smoking, and carrying on whether I did it or not, why not have a little fun? Some of my friends at school were "wild girls." It would be easy enough to join in some of their rebellion.

But something held me back. Perhaps it was pride. Maybe it was God's protection. But I just couldn't bear the thought of having Mama find out. I determined that I was going to prove Aunt Pearl wrong. "I am a Coles," I told myself, "and I am not that kind of person."

And so I continued as the kid who seldom did anything wrong. Classmates called me "goody two-shoes" and "granny goodwitch." But I was proving something to the voices in my mind. It wasn't the thick Southern voices choked with hate that kept echoing in my mind. It was a husky voice with the snap of a black woman that I fought to disprove. And so when classmates pointed a bottle my way, inviting me to take a drink, my hand would not reach out to take it. I was tempted, but I would not allow myself to numb my raw hurt with its power.

Avoiding the party scene during high school protected me from a lot more than just Pearl's wrath. It also earned the respect and attention of two white girls, Beth and Martha. About the only times white and black kids mixed at our integrated school was when we were forced to sit in alphabetical order. That was how I, Kay Coles, came to sit between Beth Boswell and Martha Delaney.

Beth and Martha were bosom buddies. Seating charts had placed them together since elementary school when they would call each other up on the phone and plan their matching outfits for the next day. When I was first assigned to sit between them, they tried to carry on their normal conversations by leaning either forward or backward in their seats. I'd feign indifference as I tasted every morsel of their whispered words. I was curious to hear what white girls talked about when they confided to one another. I was surprised to learn that their conversations sounded an awful lot like talks between black girls: "Did you see what Todd is wearing today?! Jenny is trying out for cheerleading! Can you believe that fat girl is going to put on one of those skirts?" Of course, black girls wouldn't be talking about their plans for joining the cheerleading squad, or the band for that matter. We weren't allowed.

Martha would say just about anything in front of me. She didn't curtail her conversations at all in my presence. She would lean her freckled arm on my desk and talk directly to Beth, pausing her voice only when the teacher scolded her for talking. At first I thought that this may be a sign that Martha liked me, but I came to realize that in her mind, I was just like the desk, a piece of furniture in the way. It never entered her mind to guard her speech in front of me, because it also never entered her mind that a *person* was listening.

Beth, however, seemed always aware of my presence, though she didn't quite know what to make of me. One day, out of the corner of my eye, I caught Beth studying me as we finished our geometry. My faced flushed hot, and I was glad for my caramel color that didn't broadcast to the world when I was flustered, like the red-faced white kids. I kept my gaze straight ahead and pretended not to notice. Then, in the next period, she passed me a note. I was used to accepting notes from Beth and passing them to Martha, and vice versa, but this was different. It was addressed to me! My eyes locked on the bubbly letters spelling out my name: Kay. There it was, no confusing it with Martha. I shot a glance over in Beth's direction to see what kind of game she was playing, but there was no mischievous look in her eye as she scribbled down notes from the blackboard.

Inside she wrote, "Hi! Isn't this class boring? I like your dress. —Beth." I couldn't believe it. Beth Boswell had sent me a note! Not only that, she had paid me a compliment. I was vaguely aware of an amazed Martha on the other side of me trying to read what Beth had written.

I quickly refolded the note so that a blank space faced up and wrote back, "Hi! Thanks for the note. If you think this class is bad, I heard we're doing opera again in music class!—Kay." Not to be outdone, Martha soon wrote me a note. As she passed me the note, she caught my gaze and looked deeply into my eyes. I swear that it was the first time that she had ever taken notice of me. I think it surprised her to see a person looking back at her through those dark eyes.

And so began a friendship among the three of us. We chatted away during class and passed notes when the teachers got after us for talking. We sat together in library, even though there were no assigned seats, and did our homework together on the wide tables. Beth and Martha were the first white people I had ever spent enough time with to really get a good look at their faces. Their noses were thin and pointy and sprinkled with freckles. Beth had long, flowing hair that was a golden corn color on top but darker, almost brown, underneath. Martha had dark, curly tresses that frizzed up when the rain caught her without a hat. She was covered with freckles from head to toe, and I was tempted to ask her, though I never did, if we could play connect-the-dots on her arms.

We would compare our homework and help each other out if one of us had skipped an assignment. During these times, Beth and Martha would fill me in on any news that had developed after school the day before, for they were always over at one another's house after school let out. I considered it only a matter of time before they trusted me to be a part of their after-school play. I knew that soon they would invite me over for their slumber parties, or to go horseback riding with their families on weekends. I remember one Monday morning when Beth came in our homeroom class in an excited swirl. She could hardly wait to tell me about the weekend they had had at the beach.

"Oh, Kay, we had such a wonderful time! You should have seen Martha trying to jump over the waves with me. And we ate cotton candy on the boardwalk—it was like eating sweet spider webs!" And then she would plop down in her seat, breathless in her excitement at reliving their magical weekend. I held my breath as she finished her delicious description, waiting for her to add, "Kay, you just must come with us next time!"

But it never came. I was never invited to share in their fun times.

At first it hurt me, and then it made me angry. And then I accepted the fact that we could be good friends at school but not after school hours. I wouldn't know such feelings of hurt and rejection again until I joined an integrated church.

7

God's Beloved Child

I was on familiar terms with God, having grown up accustomed to hearing my mother call upon His name almost daily. God was a kindly old grandfather figure who swept in and out of our lives at key moments like birth, baptism, marriage, and death. But I wasn't much of a pray-er, except when I was in trouble, and then I could be quite eloquent. Aunt Pearl made sure that she, J. B., and I went to Mount Carmel

Baptist Church once a quarter whether we needed to or not.

Inside the walls of the church, I heard that I was God's beloved child, created in His image. Knowing this made me feel like I was a valuable and cherished child. The church also taught me that hate destroys the human spirit, but love builds it up. Part of the magnetic draw of the black church was the warm fellowship. It was one of very few places where "our kind" could go to find love, acceptance, and that most scarce of all commodities, respect.

I loved those Sundays when the choir director included a gospel tune with a snatch of African percussion. As a melancholy child, those "nobody knows the trouble I seen" songs spoke to my heart. But my favorite songs were those that enticed the usually reserved congregation to keep time with foot stomps and claps. When the choir was especially good, the ladies of the church would add a little hop to their clap and the men would open their hands wide apart on every clap and rock back and forth with the pulse. We'd wear out the lyrics, singing them five or six times through until the congregation had worked itself into a frenzy of singing and clapping. Then it would be over and the men would hitch up their pants a notch or two, and the ladies would fan their glowing faces, and the whole church would settle into the pews with a satisfied and exhausted *Amen*.

The older I became, however, the less sense I could make of what I heard and saw in church. I thought long and hard about the porcelain Jesus hanging limply from the cross on the wall. It often caused my little mind to question how a blue-eyed, blond Jesus could love dark, nappy me. Would there be a separate section in heaven, in the back near the edge separating heaven from hell, for us blacks?

The whole business about being a Christian also confused me. In tightly knit communities like ours, everybody knows everybody else's business. It puzzled me that many of those who sang, professed, confessed, and preached on Sunday lived rather unchristian lives the rest of the week. By the time I entered my senior year of high school, I had pretty much decided that Christianity was a great set of rules to govern your life, but that was it. I was a good kid, I always had been, and if God graded on the curve, I'd surely get into heaven.

One evening, J. B., Pearl, and I sat around the kitchen table, eating dinner with the television droning on in the background as it usually did during meals. The show caught my attention.

I forgot to eat and sat with my eyes glued to the screen.

"That guy have anything *interesting* to say?" my uncle asked. He was referring to Billy Graham, whose earnest face filled the television screen.

"Mmmm," I replied, concentrating on what Dr. Graham was saying. I'd dialed past televised crusades before without much interest. But this time it seemed that he was talking directly to me! He was speaking to young people about confusion, loneliness, alienation, and fear.

"Do you feel an emptiness in your heart? A lack of purpose and meaning in your life?"

"Yes," I whispered in my heart.

"There is a place in our soul that only Jesus Christ can fill," he explained. I had definitely felt that emptiness!

"Going to church doesn't make you a Christian any more than going to a garage makes you a car," he said. *Wow!* I thought to myself. *Then what* does *make you a Christian?* Just as if he were reading my mind, Dr. Graham started talking about our need to turn our lives over to Jesus Christ, who would help us be the kind of person we wanted to be.

It sounded great, but I didn't know what it meant to "give my life to Christ." It sounded sort of scary. After dinner I went to my room and prayed. Billy Graham seemed so trustworthy, and I imagined that God would be something like him. I told God that I would give my life to Him for a year, to see what would happen.

There weren't any lightning bolts or emotional feelings. I certainly didn't feel any different. I found a Bible and began reading a few chapters every night. I couldn't think of anyone I could share my decision with, so I kept it to myself and studied and prayed on my own. It wasn't long before I noticed changes in myself. I was less concerned with rules and being "perfect" and more concerned with pleasing God. When I did something wrong, I felt a sorrow deep in my heart. Most of all, I had a sense of peace, a calm and a confidence that I had never experienced. It wasn't long before others remarked on the different person I was becoming. I wanted to tell them, "That's because I'm a Christian now," but I never could say it.

8

The Radical Years

The warm fellowship I experienced in the black church ignited within me a desire to attend a historically black college. It was important for me to go to a college where I was not a minority, somewhere where people understood me, my background, my hair. I wanted to go to a college where I could join the pep squad, the sororities, or the math club if I wanted to.

Not that I had all that much choice. In 1967 there were some opportunities to go to white institutions—not as many as today, but there were a few. Nevertheless, my first choice in schools was Hampton University, where I enrolled as a history major. At Hampton, the black power, black pride, and black-is-beautiful movements were in full blossom.

My discovery and celebration of my black identity paralleled my discovery and celebration of my identity as a beloved child of God. Up until then, I was quite sure that I was the only one around who was serious about getting to know Jesus. It shocked me one day to overhear some students discussing Jesus' command: "... Go and make disciples of all nations." Not only were there others like me who were serious about this Christian thing, but they were pretty normal-looking kids—not at all the geeks I had expected to find poring over the Bible.

I joined the InterVarsity Christian Fellowship (IVCF) on campus. I couldn't get enough of the Bible studies and prayer meetings that the IVCF staff led with Hampton students.

My growing knowledge of the Bible led me to a greater understanding of who I am in God's eyes. One of my favorite passages during this period was Psalm 139, especially the lines that read:

For you created my inmost being;
You knit me together in my mother's womb.

I praise you because I am fearfully
and wonderfully made;
Your works are wonderful,
I know that full well.

I am fearfully and wonderfully made! I would tell myself over and over again. God had knit me together in my mother's womb. He loved me even before I was born!

It dawned on me that not only had God created me, but He had created me black. A newfound pride in being black sprouted within me and within several of the Christians on campus. We knew that black is beautiful, and we knew why. God had created us in His image, and God did not create mistakes. He knew what He was doing when He gave us kinky hair, broad noses, full lips, and darker skin. These were beautiful physical features, not traits to be camouflaged in an effort to appear more white.

During this phase we threw away the bleaching creams we had used in high school to make our skin lighter and the processing chemicals to straighten our hair. Both the men and the women in our clique wore their hair in a curly mass known as an "afro." We affectionately termed our hairdo a "natural," because it was naturally who we are. Kinte cloth wasn't big then, but if it had been, I would probably have gone to class looking like an African village queen.

We fellow black Christians had a saying that summed up our theology: "We're not a minority, we're a chosen few." We "chosen few" made it our business to ensure that we didn't remain few. We learned how to share our faith in Jesus Christ with other students on campus. The fact that Hampton students were culled mostly from the Bible Belt made things harder instead of easier. It is difficult for someone who has been brought up knowing only *about* God to become interested in knowing God.

The rise in power and prominence of Black Muslims also made our efforts to tell people about Jesus more difficult. Malcolm X and his followers had labeled Christianity "the white man's religion." Those who followed Christ were looked down upon as having sold out to the white establishment. The militants argued that since white America had made itself rich on our backs, it owed us something. Seeing that the "white devils" would never give us anything willingly, we were going to have to take it—by any means necessary.

Although I did not agree with their solutions to the turmoil in our nation, I could certainly understand why their message of black power had vast appeal for those who felt alienated in America. Their beliefs were built on hate, bitterness, and in some cases, I think, fear. I heard Jesus calling for us to forgive and move toward racial reconciliation. To the black militants, "love" and "forgiveness" seemed a show of cowardly weakness. In my mind, if black Americans worked to establish justice for all, it would be the most awesome display of power and love ever witnessed in America.

After being graduated, a friend of mine who worked for the telephone company let me know that they were hiring. I must have interviewed well because they were puzzled as to why I was applying for an operator's slot. I mumbled, "I thought that's all I was qualified to do around here." The interviewer suggested that I was qualified for a management position, and would I be interested? Within a week I was hired as a manager at C&P Telephone Company.

I found the office environment exhilarating. My co-workers didn't seem too shocked to be working with, and sometimes under, a black female. There were very few instances where my race or gender even cropped up as an issue.

I was amazed that a company was actually seeking out black college graduates. Corporate

America was waking up and realizing that there was an untapped pool of talent out there. Let's not say that they woke up on their own. A few thousand lawsuits helped open their eyes. In fact, many firms were trying to protect themselves from those lawsuits by aggressively trying to hire minorities.

I had not been in the job very long before I was promoted and offered a transfer to Roanoke, Virginia, an area that we not so fondly referred to as the "sticks." One of the women in the office said in a voice that was obviously for my hearing, "I guess you have to be a Negro to go anywhere in this company today." I shot back at her without even thinking: "No, you just have to be good." But there was an element of truth in what she said at the time, and I resented it. I guess I spent a good portion of my professional career trying to prove that I was hired because I was capable of doing my job well, not just because I'm black.

Determined to prove people like that woman wrong, I accepted the promotion and packed my bags for unknown territory. I spent my savings on a professional wardrobe, and after a quick good-bye to my family, I left for Roanoke.

9

Work and Marriage

My college roommate was from Roanoke, and she introduced me to my future husband my first day in there. Earlier in the day, Sharon just happened to run across a friend of hers and said, "Charles, why don't you come by? I want you to meet somebody tonight."

When Sharon told me that she had invited a "good buddy" of hers to meet me, I balked—"Don't even think what you're thinking." The last thing I needed, I thought, was a Cupid.

I met Charles that night. He disliked me immediately, and I felt the same way about him.

It took me two seconds after seeing him amble in the door to classify him as a "Roanoke hick." He thought that I was a Richmond snob. He later made a comment to one of his friends that if it had rained that night, I would have surely drowned because my nose was so stuck up in the air. He was a motorcycle-riding, long-haired guy who hadn't finished college.

But before he even met me, Charles had promised Sharon that he would take me to dinner the following day for my birthday. Despite his immediate dislike for me, he kept his promise. So there we were the next night, gritting our teeth through what began as an extremely uncomfortable date. Then something happened. I noticed that although he hadn't finished school, Charles was the brightest, most articulate man I had ever met.

I found myself hoping that he would ask me out again. I wasn't disappointed. We were soon inseparable. He was the best friend I ever had. It didn't take long for us to realize that we were falling in love.

Our wedding was a simple ceremony performed within a year of our first meeting. We didn't have much money for a honeymoon so we thought we ought to go somewhere relatively cheap. Charles suggested Manhattan. Where did we get the idea that New York City was cheap? We couldn't even afford a room-service breakfast at our hotel. We also didn't realize how cold it can get in New York in January. It was freezing. Walking to the theater district was out of the question and we hadn't planned on the expense of taxis, so we pretty much stayed in our hotel room the whole time.

One of the first things we did once we settled in was try to find a church that we both liked. We tried many black churches and loved the music and fellowship. But both of us had a strong hunger for more biblical teaching and less "entertainment." On a lark, we dropped by a white church that one of our IVCF friends from college had recommended, Grace Church. It had everything we were looking for, except black folks. And that was a major obstacle. This was 1974, and 11:00 A.M. Sunday was still the most segregated hour in America

On our first visit we provoked many stares and whispers. The pastor greeted us warmly at the door and introduced us to a few members of the congregation who, after an initial bout of shock, welcomed us. It became clear that the church was willing to try integration if we were. Were we?

After much prayer and hand-wringing we

chose spiritual growth over comfort, and joined. Once the church leadership recognized Charles's biblical knowledge, which now was combined with solid faith, they elected him as a deacon. But our time at Grace was not without racial slights. I became involved in a weekly women's Bible study. One of the highlights of the year was a family trip to Myrtle Beach. All year long, references to the annual family beach trip were dropped into conversation. I had heard so many stories about the fun times they had together that I was really looking forward to going. But we were never invited. As summer drew near, I overheard women making arrangements for shared beach houses, but the conversation would die down whenever I came near. The group left for the beach without us, and I was crushed. I'd never felt so betrayed and rejected.

Eventually my hurt died down enough for me to ask why we had not been included in the beach trip. An uncomfortable silence fell upon the room. "Well, Kay, we just felt that—well you know that there aren't very many black people at Myrtle Beach ... and we just thought you would be uncomfortable." They were concerned for *us*? It took all my courage just to read a Scripture verse out loud before the group, but I wanted to say something else. I did. "I guess I thought that if we wouldn't be accepted at a certain vacation spot, that you would choose another one rather than leave us out." Nothing more was ever said about it.

* * *

On the job I was learning valuable skills in management. Two of the principles I learned are the importance of a sense of humor and the power of not losing your cool. Once, when I supervised the Directory Assistance office, one of the black operators received an obnoxious caller who threatened, "Listen, you better give me that number!" She tried very hard to find the number but couldn't. He demanded to speak to her supervisor, so she put me on the line, warning me that this was a live one.

"Can I help you, sir?" I asked in my sweetest voice. A gruff voice on the other end barked at me, "Can you get me that number? That stupid nigger wouldn't give it to me." I said, "Well, sir, this one can't either because the number is not published." He hung up.

My life as a career woman was taking off. I became a force manager for long distance, and I was really enjoying work. We discussed starting a family, but then there was talk of giving me another promotion, and we decided to put off having children until I had plateaued at work. But it was too late. I was pregnant.

We had already made the decision that when we had children, one of us would stay home with them. We had talked with other young black couples about the trends we saw with the black family. Somebody had to be giving full attention to the children. Charles was not the nurturer. He also didn't have the ability to nurse. So we made the decision that I would come home.

In June of 1974, Charles Everett James, Jr. came into the world with a shriek, and he continued to cry for about nine months straight. I had a very colicky child. He was a clutchy, clinging baby who would cry if I went out of his sight. Chuck was such a demanding baby that I really couldn't enjoy the benefits of being home and raising a baby. A dark cloud hovered. Chuck never slept more than a couple of hours at night. When he awakened, he screamed. Both Charles and I were physically worn out.

Eventually a compassion squad from the church came to rescue us. A few women would take turns spending the night with us, getting up to take care of Chuck so that Charles and I could get some sleep. From day one, I never had to ask Charles to change a diaper or feed one of the children or give a bath. There may be difficult issues in our marriage, but that's never been one of them. His career with C&P was taking off. While I couldn't get it together at home, he was coming home telling me about his business lunches and all the neat places he had been. I grew resentful and angry. But at least I saw a light at the end of the tunnel. When he turned nine months old, Chuck began to quiet down a little.

And then, rather unexpectedly, we found ourselves expecting another child. My only daughter—Elizabeth—the sunshine of my life. Three years later, we had another pleasant surprise with my pride and joy, Robbie, our third child.

The timing of my becoming pregnant with Elizabeth was not good. Physically I was weak, and emotionally I was a wreck. Still, I learned a valuable lesson from that experience, *an unwanted pregnancy is not an unwanted child.* All three of my pregnancies have been mistimed and unplanned, and yet all three of my children have been cherished additions to the family.

The second lesson I learned was that to pull through, women in crisis pregnancies need the help and support of their family and community. I really needed the folks from our church to come over and have an adult conversation with me, to watch Chuck one morning a week so that I could run errands, to pass along baby clothes.

One morning a woman from church told me of her involvement with a crisis pregnancy center called *Birthright*. She let us know that they needed volunteers. She explained that a number of the women who called in were black and that it would be very nice to have some black counselors who could make these young women feel more comfortable. So I would pack up Chuck a few days a week and take him with me to the *Birthright* center to answer phones or stuff envelopes in between calls. That was my first exposure to the issue. I was horrified at what I learned and saw. I knew instinctively that killing an unborn baby was wrong, but I had never studied it as an issue. When I began to read the literature and see the pictures and as I became more educated about the issue, I felt very deeply about it.

I continued my volunteer work at *Birthright* until the call we had been waiting for came through, and Charles was promoted to Richmond.

10

Melted Butter and Hardened Clay

My mother moved in with us and she spent her day cleaning our house until the floors shone. Charles and the kids weren't used to kitchen floors that didn't stick and ironed socks, but they soon adjusted. Her help gave me a lot more free time. Determined not to let that free time get sponged up by the afternoon soaps, I set out on my first project, to help my father receive help for his alcoholism.

First, I needed to find him. He and my

mother had stopped speaking years before, but in recent years he had cut off almost all contact with his kids as well. He had remarried and lived somewhere on the east side of town. One day one of my brothers ran into him at a car dealership, where he worked as a janitor. I tracked him down. I had checked into all the drug and alcohol treatment centers available. There wasn't much, and what was available was incredibly expensive.

Unfortunately, one of my brothers was following right in my father's footsteps. Lucky, one of the middle children, had become the type of alcoholic that drank wine out of a dirty paper sack as he sat on park benches with his friends. I would drive around at night, poking through alleys and parks, looking for him. I'd drag an inebriated Lucky into the backseat where he'd stretch out and sleep. At home we'd let him shower and shave and fix himself up, and he'd leave the house the next morning, promising that he wouldn't touch any alcohol that day. He was going to look for a job. And then every night I'd search the parks and alleys for him to bring him home again.

I continued these search-and-rescue missions for my brother and father for about six months before my heart grew sick. It wasn't the string of lies and broken promises that disheartened me; it was the trauma of having to see them in such a low state, day after day. I just backed off entirely. Eventually, Lucky responded to treatment and has been clean and sober for more than ten years. My father's alcoholism eventually killed him.

When I finally acknowledged to myself that there was little more I could do for my father, I began to look around for part-time volunteer work. I was looking for something that would empower the black community. Charles and I became testers with a fair-housing project. We would go in and try to buy or rent property to see if we were being discriminated against as blacks. Boy, did that experience ever open my eyes!

I can remember one assignment in particular. I went into the rental office, dressed very well. The woman behind the counter was very friendly and made chitchat as she searched her paperwork to see if they had any two-bedroom apartments available. She looked genuinely sad as she told me that there were no openings at the time. "Why don't you check back after the end of the month?" She added as I left, "We often have more openings then."

As I walked back to the car, I saw a couple of little black kids building sand castles in the playground sandbox. *No discrimination here*, I thought. When I reached the car around the corner, I didn't say anything and let the white tester go in. It grew hot and humid sitting in the car. I couldn't imagine what was taking him so long. It only took me about ten minutes more to get my answer. When he strolled out after thirty minutes and got in the car, I asked, "Bruce, what took you so long? I've been melting in this car!"

"I don't know how you got through those two empty apartments so fast," he replied. I stared at him blankly. "You have to be kidding," I said testily. "No ... Didn't she show them to you?" That's when I realized two things about race in America. First, despite laws and much progress, racism still exists in America. It's just more subtle. The second thing I realized is that quotas are no easy answer. That woman felt safe in turning me away because she had her quota of blacks in the complex, and she wasn't accepting any more. That scenario was repeated over and over again during the time that Charles and I were testers.

* * *

When we left Grace Church in Roanoke, many in the congregation suggested that we try Stoneypoint, a sister Presbyterian church in

Richmond. We did, hoping to find at least a handful of black families in the congregation. There were none, but we couldn't walk away from the teaching, fellowship, and evangelism that we found there. At Stoneypoint we met several folks fired up about the issue of abortion. A small group began praying about what sort of help we could provide. We decided to set up a Crisis Pregnancy Center to reach out to pregnant women in need of assistance.

Very often as I talked with young women at the Crisis Pregnancy Center, they would say, "I'm having this abortion because I feel like I have no other choice." Sometimes the baby's father had left, offering no support. Many girls were afraid to let their parents know that they were pregnant. Other times a single parent with one or two children saw no hope of being able to manage yet another child. I discovered that if one sat down with each woman and provided her with some alternatives so that she had an option other than abortion—the overwhelming majority chose life.

Because I had three young children of my own at that point, my volunteer activity was limited. But Charles and I had our name on the list of supporters and were often called upon to open our home to a pregnant woman, or a woman and her baby. We had several women come to live with us. Sometimes it was a young pregnant girl who needed somewhere to live; other times it was a new mother and her baby. I huffed and blew my way through several deliveries as a Lamaze coach.

It was during this time that I was also forced to come to terms with my relationship with my aunt and uncle. J. B. died unexpectedly. I was angry at him for leaving. He had been a loving and stable force in an otherwise turbulent childhood. A few bitter feelings lingered about his not standing up for me, but as I learned more about alcoholism, I realized that nonconfrontation was his way of dealing with my aunt. My aunt died three years later. I wasn't angry at her for leaving. From the time I was a teenager, Pearl and I enjoyed a warm and affectionate friendship when she was sober, but I had learned early on in life to avoid her when she had been with a bottle.

I sat by the bed and held her hand the night she passed away. I just kept telling her, "It's okay. It's okay." I wanted her to know that I forgave her for all the jibes and anger she had directed at me in her alcoholic state. The night that she passed wasn't an appropriate time to be angry. It was a time for forgiveness and reconciliation.

They say that the same sun that melts the butter, hardens the clay. During my childhood, certain things had been as constant as the rising and setting of the sun. My father's neglect, my aunt's alcoholism, the heat of poverty and, racism, and the emotional abuse from my aunt could have made me very soft and needy, or very bitter and hard. I melted. I spent all of my life trying to prove to my aunt that I wasn't the loose, no-good, nasty girl she thought I was. And I still catch myself trying to do that as I try to please and win approval. I've spent most of my adult life trying to learn what made me react with softening rather than hardening. It's still a mystery.

11

Amazing Grace

"How can Jesus come in your heart?" asked our three-and-a-half-year-old daughter, Bizzie. Good question. "When we say 'come into my heart,' we mean that we've asked Jesus to help us live the way that God wants us to and to stay with us all the time. Bizzie, Jesus wants every single one of His children to follow Him. Do you want to ask Jesus into your heart?"

After a few rare moments of quiet, Bizzie said with a smile that she had asked Jesus "to come live in my heart." That simple declaration of faith came back as a reassuring blanket the night a few months later when I stood beside Bizzie's hospital bed and saw her heart monitor fall to a flat line.

* * *

I was worried about Bizzie. She had been sick for weeks. During the day she seemed perfectly normal, but at night her temperature shot up so high that she became delirious. The doctors didn't seem too concerned, but they hadn't seen Bizzie at night, her sheets drenched with sweat, mumbling and crying that her head hurt. Her fevers spiked up to 103º and 104º. After one particularly bad Saturday night, I was in a panic. I felt my little girl slipping out of my reach.

"This is not the flu!" I practically yelled at the doctor. "You've got to find out what's going on! This has gone on too long." He finally agreed. Bizzie was admitted to the hospital to run a series of tests.

Within three days of being admitted to the hospital, I realized that Bizzie was slipping away from us. My bouncy and playful child was alternately lethargic and aggressive. She was going through long periods during which she was incoherent and didn't seem to recognize those in the room with her. She rarely spoke, but when she did it was like a broken record: "Mommy, I'm cold. Mommy, my head hurts." But I was helpless. The doctors couldn't diagnose her illness, and since they did not know what was wrong, they couldn't treat her. I began spending nights at the hospital.

All of her charts and all of the expressions on the doctors' faces told us that she was dying. Every day she lost another function, another sign of the life within. First she stopped walking, then she stopped eating. Then she slept all the time. Finally, she slipped into a coma.

We rejoiced when a visiting doctor came who was able to diagnose Bizzie's strange illness. He studied her charts and after examining her for only two minutes declared: "She's got tuberculin meningitis." My heart leaped. We finally knew what was wrong with her!

"What do we need to do? How bad is it?" we asked, full of hope.

"It's pretty bad. When the disease runs its course, it's usually fatal within three weeks," he said and walked out the door with Bizzie's charts. My heart sank. He held out no sign of hope, no consoling words. Just the facts. Three weeks.

But at least now we knew what we were dealing with, and we knew specifically how to pray. But we also felt dread at a disease that was so devastating. Basically, tuberculin meningitis is tuberculosis that, instead of settling on the lungs as it usually does, settles on the brain covering. So it wasn't in her lungs, it was in her brain.

Just when we needed them most, folks from our church sprang into action to help. The house was a mess. There was nothing in the refrigerator except limp celery, curdled milk, and a package of hot dogs. Someone loaned us a car so I could drive to and from the hospital. Others cooked meals and cleaned our house, baby-sat the boys, and donated money to help cover the hospital bills.

One evening as we were preparing Bizzie for the night, Charles moved her legs, and was shocked to notice they were as stiff as a board. I lifted her foot and her entire body came off the bed. We realized that she was having a seizure. Charles pushed the emergency bell and called for a nurse. She took one look at Bizzie and then looked up at her heart monitor with a gasp. It was a flat line. My baby's heart had stopped! All heaven broke loose. The emergency heart team wheeled their cart into the room and pushed us out the door. The hospital chaplain, a Catholic nun, was on hand almost as soon as the resuscitation unit. She walked us out of the room, explaining that they needed all the room they could get to try to resuscitate Bizzie. The three

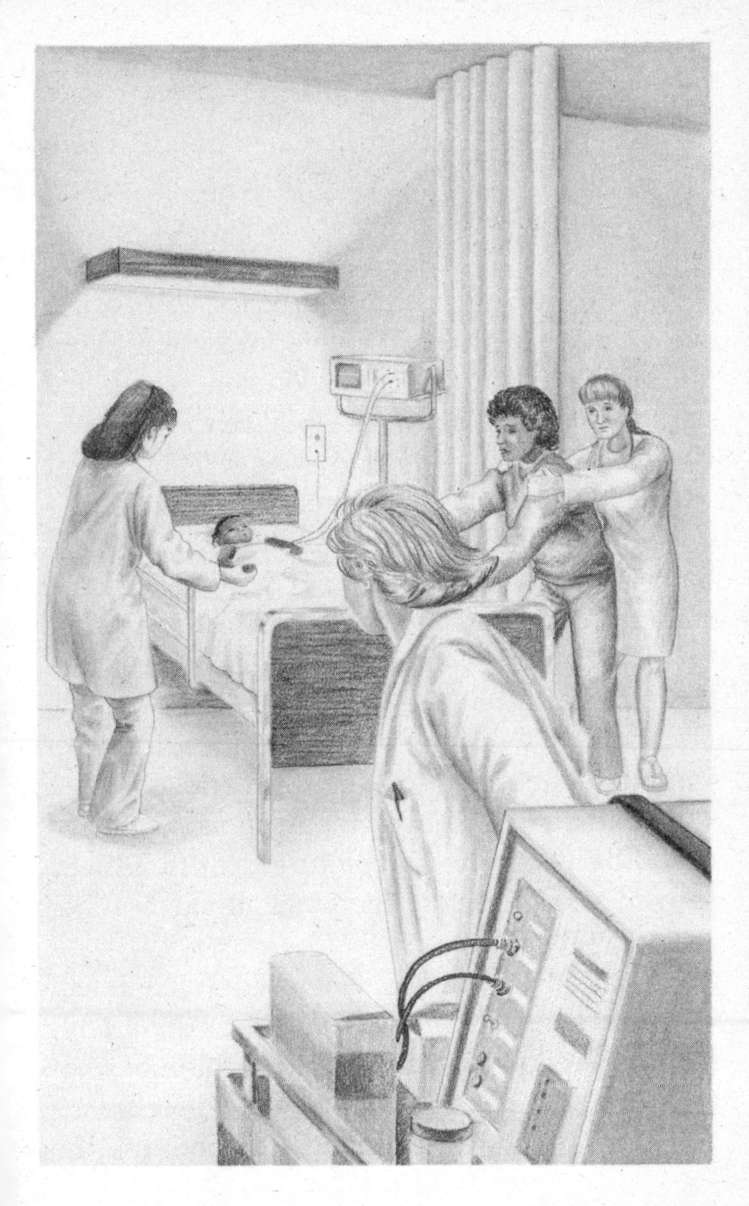

of us walked numbly down the hall to the waiting room.

We prayed until the resuscitation team came out of the room. Of course we all looked at Dr. Bundy's face to see if it was over.

"I'm sorry," he said, "This was unanticipated. We have been able to stabilize her, but she cannot stay here. It's very important to get her to the Medical College of Virginia. I think you might want to go see her before we move her." I could discern that Dr. Bundy was still afraid that we could lose her at any minute. He tried to prepare us for what we would see when we went back into the room. "She's not going to look the same," he warned. He described all of the various machines and tubes that had been inserted. He explained that they had ripped her clothes off her and that she was spread-eagled with something attached to every arm and leg.

Nothing could have prepared us for what we saw. She was a horror picture. Her head was shaved and she had a metal shunt stuck in her brain.

I asked Dr. Bundy if she could hear us. "Hearing is one of the last senses to go. If anything, she can hear you." I tried to think of what I would say to her. I thought back to our conversation in the car a few months before, and the most comforting thing I could think of to say was that Jesus was with her and that He would be with her forever. "Jesus will never leave you," I whispered in her tiny ear. "Nothing can separate us from God's love. Nothing."

Later that night at the new, better-equipped hospital, her new team of doctors sat us down and prepared us for the worst. "She's alive," they said, "but we don't know what the quality of her life will be even if she survives." They told us that her brain had been without oxygen, and it had taken sufficiently long to revive her—that we were probably looking at severe brain damage. Tears streamed down my face as I thought of Bizzie as a "vegetable." Providentially, a friend was on hand to remind me that even if Bizzie came through her ordeal physically or mentally handicapped, she was still my daughter, and we would still celebrate her life.

* * *

We had sort of forgotten about Christmas. It was intentional forgetting, I suppose. It just didn't seem right to be celebrating and singing carols, with Bizzie so sick. It was the week before Christmas and our house had no tree, no decorations, and we hadn't bought any presents because we had no money. Again, the church body rallied around us. I came home one night from the hospital, dead tired and depressed, and the entire house was awash with red velvet ribbon, pine boughs, and angels. The youth group had bought a tree and brought it over and decorated it for us. There were presents underneath for everyone in the family. Chuck was thrilled, I cried again, and Charles stared misty-eyed at our transformed house. The Christmas spirit began to infuse our spirits in spite of the circumstances.

I was hanging out in the hospital corridor when the nurse came looking for me. She wore an intense look. My stomach knotted up. "Is this the end?" I wondered, but she broke into an uncharacteristic smile. "I want to show you something." I practically ran to Bizzie's room. She lay in her bed snuggled next to her blanket. "Watch this," said the nurse, snatching Bizzie's blanket away from her face, laying it just outside her fingers. Bizzie grabbed it back. I almost fainted. Her eyes were still closed, she still seemed lost, but she had moved!

"Bizzie ... Honey ... Biz!" I called. Her eyes flickered open. "Where's my mommy?" she asked.

"Here I am, baby!" And I kissed her dry, cracked lips. She looked confused. I held her tiny, frail hands as she looked around the room taking in her surroundings. She looked at all the tubes and wires coming out of her body. She felt her bald head. Then she turned to me and said, "Can I have some peanut-butter cookies?"

I climbed next to Bizzie on her bed and pulled her close to my heart. We rocked back and forth and I whispered, "Thank you, Lord. Thank you, Lord," until I was hoarse.

It took me three tries to get the dime into the pay phone. Finally I got Charles on the line and told him that our daughter had "come back" and that she wanted some peanut-butter cookies, and that I was going home to bake them. He thought this was a great idea. We'd meet back at the hospital. Everyone else thought I had flipped.

Back at home I had the phone under my chin letting everyone know the good news as I stirred cookie dough with my hands. As soon as the first batch was done, I carefully wrapped them in a Christmas box and raced the car back to the hospital. It was a glorious next couple of days. All of our friends from church who had been so helpful throughout the ordeal rejoiced with us in our good news.

Eventually the day came when she was released from the hospital. Her muscles had atrophied to the point that she couldn't walk, crawl, or even hold her head up. A long rehabilitation process began. We didn't know if any long-term physical impairments would linger. I guess we knew that the horror was over one day in March. I had bundled her up and set her on a lawn chair out front so that she could watch her brother ride his bicycle. Knowing that she couldn't move, Chuck teased her by getting on her tricycle and peddling down the driveway. I shook my head at my son's cruelty as I watched from the picture window. To Chuck's amazement, Bizzie pulled herself off of the lawn chair and onto the grass. She slowly and painfully pulled herself upright, walked down the driveway, and popped Chuck right on the nose. Then she got up on her tricycle and slowly pedaled it back up the driveway. She angrily bundled herself back up and sat down on the lawn chair.

A year later, Bizzie was completely recovered. Her hair grew back. She grew in strength. Her scars faded. But not all. One bedsore on Bizzie's heel became badly infected. It formed a callus and then a deep scar that is still with her today. We call it her "ebenezer." In Old Testament times, the people of God would build a pile of stones to indicate the places in their lives where God had performed a miracle. When their children and others saw the pile of stones, called an *ebenezer*, they would naturally ask what the symbol represented. It provided the believer with an opportunity to give a testimony of the act that God had performed.

12

Washington, D.C.

From the porch-sitting, lemonade-sipping South we moved to the hustle-bustle, here's-my-business-card North.

Perhaps the biggest culture shock was the food. Our local supermarket didn't even carry chitterlings or pigs' feet, so occasionally Charles and I would get our soul-food fix at the Florida Avenue Grill in D.C.

When I had gone in to resign from Circuit City in Richmond, I was given a promotion and assigned to the regional headquarters in Beltsville, Maryland. We were ecstatic! We knew that the cost of living meant that I would have to work, and now I had found a job without even looking!

And then someone from the National Right to Life Committee called to say that a black cable-television program was interested in doing a talk show on the abortion issue. They wanted me to represent the pro-life position. I laughed and said, "Thank you, but no way. Nope. But thanks for calling," and quickly hung up.

However when I told Charles and the kids about the unusual phone call, Chuck looked very disappointed. "Why don't you want to help save all those unborn babies?" he asked. Charles suggested that I call them back the next day. And I did, hoping that they had found someone else. But they hadn't.

The show aired live during prime time. To say that I was scared to death is an understatement. I hadn't slept the night before, and I hadn't eaten all day. All I could think about as they hooked me up to the wireless mike was how awful it would be if I threw up in front of all those cameras and they caught the sound on my mike.

I debated a woman associated with Planned Parenthood. My opponent was a seasoned veteran, well-armed with statistics and polls. I felt like David going up against Goliath. Despite my insecurity, the show went very well.

As they took off the mike that night, the tension and anxiety that had haunted me ever since the phone call ebbed away. I looked forward to falling back into anonymity in my role as mother and manager. But the Lord had other plans. Soon after the show aired, the executive director of the National Right to Life Committee called and offered me a job. I didn't want to take it. I had a wonderful job in corporate America that was allowing our family to live beyond the just-scraping-by routine. But then I became convicted in my heart that while this battle for the lives of millions of unborn children was going on all around me, I could not hide myself behind a good job selling stereos and TV sets.

That began a whirlwind three years of debating, giving speeches, holding press conferences, and traveling at home and abroad almost nonstop. My travel schedule was so hectic that I was on the road more than I was home.

I was exhausted but exhilarated at the progress we were making. I knew that I was a success when Faye Wattleton, the formidable spokesperson for Planned Parenthood, refused to debate me.

Debates offered us the best opportunity to

present our case without those in the media (who tend to be very pro-abortion) distorting our message. I felt enormous pressure to debate well; to be clear, creative, and concise. I learned to trust God for wisdom and even for the very words I would speak. Two hours before we were due to go on stage, I would lock myself in my hotel room with the phone off the hook and "eat rug." "Eating rug" means to pray in the most humbling position possible—lying prone with your face down on the floor. From that vantage point I would confess to God my inadequacies and my fears. And I would ask Him to speak His words through me.

After one debate I returned to my dark and lonely hotel room and called home. Robbie's six-year-old voice whined into the phone, "Mommy, why won't you come home?" That was the beginning of the end for me. I decided that if I saved every unborn child in America and lost my own, I would have failed in my life's primary mission. I thought about working part-time. And then came the heart-wrenching news that my mother was dying of cancer. I resigned from the National Right to Life.

* * *

My mother had been a servant all her life,

constantly pouring out to others. We decided that even if it caused us to go in the hole, we were going to make her last few months the most glorious ones we could give her. I temporarily moved back to Richmond to care for her. Before I headed south, I stopped in at the Bush campaign office to put in my two cents worth on a few issues close to my heart. When he heard that I was there, George Bush, Jr. stopped in to see me. We had gotten to know one another when I was campaigning for pro-life candidates, his father included, throughout the past year.

"Kay, would you consider coming on board?" he asked. I flashed him my "Come on now, be serious" look. "Really, Kay, you're a natural. Would you at least consider it?"

"No, I'm really not interested," I demurred, explaining that my mother had been diagnosed with cancer and the prognosis was not good. But it tickled me to have been asked. "How about that?" I asked myself getting into the car.

In her hospital room later on that day, I tried to encourage my mother before she went in for surgery. "You know, Mama, I had an interesting offer today. George Bush, Jr. asked me to come in and serve in the new administration! Can you imagine that! Of course I said no, but it just tickled me that he would ask." Mama wasn't smiling. Lying prone on her hospital gurney, minutes before she went in for surgery, she proceeded to bless me out as only a black woman can do.

"Girl, what's wrong with you! I raised you better than that! The son of the president of the United States asks you to serve your nation and you say no! How many people do you think get that kind of opportunity? How many black folks you think ben' asked?! Girl, you bes' get back on that phone and tell him you was just kidding!"

She made sure that I called campaign headquarters from her room. After they wheeled Mama out, I told George that based on my skills and abilities, I wanted to come in at as high a position as I possibly could "because I don't have a lot of time to make my mother proud."

A day or two later I was asked to head up the public affairs team at the nation's largest agency, the U.S. Department of Health and Human Services. I was so proud that I couldn't squeeze the smile off my face when I went in to tell my mother that I would be serving as the Assistant Secretary for Public Affairs. Mama looked a little disappointed: "But you can't even type!"

I explained that "Assistant Secretary" was a subcabinet position, an office with enough responsibility to require Senate confirmation.

She smiled at that. We were both looking forward to her being able to witness my swearing-in ceremony, but the confirmation process took so long that she was too weak to make the trip. She died four months later.

I loved serving a cabinet officer but the pace was grueling! The demands of my job had just about strained all of our family relationships to the limit. When an old friend called about a position with a nonprofit group dedicated to helping troubled youth, I was ready for a break. Then after just one year away, I was ready to plunge back into the world of politics as a leader in the president's fight against drug abuse. My insights on drug treatment, enforcement, and prevention came through firsthand experiences with my father and brother. The kids called me the "Drug Czarina."

Later that year I gave a brief speech at the Republican National Convention. As I mounted that massive stage to speak about family values, I remembered my own family—certainly not perfect like the Brady Bunch on TV, but a family just the same. Even when it becomes fractured or damaged by the cares of this world, it is still the unit that was meant to give each of us a sense of who we are, of who we can become.

13

A Life of Learning

As I write this final chapter, I am again in public service, this time as the Secretary of Health and Human Resources for the Commonwealth of Virginia. Many of the state's crucial programs for helping people in need are my responsibility. One of the most challenging parts of my job is deciding how to help people in need of food, money, and health care, without causing them to become dependent upon the government for these things. My opponents often accuse me of forgetting where I came from.

But I haven't forgotten. I remember the

important role of hard work, self-discipline, and taking personal responsibility in my success and the success of other blacks whose lives began in poverty. That is why I think our government programs should encourage these things.

I haven't forgotten the racial slurs, the spit in my face, or the pinpricks I faced when I integrated into the schools. I haven't forgotten being turned away from housing simply because I am black. And I most certainly haven't forgotten my childhood and the pain of going to bed hungry and cold.

But as I look back over my life as a metaphor for the survival of the black race in America, I see clearly that while government programs and court decisions played a major role in our advancement, so, too, did key values such as faith, honesty, self-reliance, perseverance, family loyalty, and responsibility. If we are to make progress against the problems that bring down our families and communities, these values must still play a leading role.

As I look back over my life, I realize that God raised me up to be a leader by giving me a life full of learning.

He began with a few lessons in humility in the slums of Portsmouth, Virginia, and then at Creighton Court in Richmond, Virginia, but the chill of poverty and alcoholism was warmed away by the love of family and neighbors who brought healing to a broken home. He blessed me with an extended family of kin and community who taught me right from wrong, and brothers who taught me pride in earning my way in this world.

Black educators imbued an expectation of excellence. In breaking the color barrier as a schoolgirl, I learned the evil of racial hatred. In college, God taught me to appreciate my heritage, to see that I am beautifully and wonderfully made. I was graduated from college with the knowledge that I am His beloved child; it was the most important thing I learned in school.

He gave me a husband whose sense of humor through all life's trials taught me resilient joy. My daughter's brush with death taught me the sanctity of life. And He gave me the opportunity to use my gifts and talents to speak for those who cannot speak for themselves: unborn children. Most of all, there was Mama, the black sheep of the family, who taught me through her life the essence of love, the importance of family, and the meaning of faith.

And I will never forget!